WAIT, SKATES!

By
MILDRED D. JOHNSON

Illustrated by
RICK STROMOSKI

Children's Press®
A Division of Scholastic Inc.
New York Toronto London Auckland Sydney
Mexico City New Delhi Hong Kong
Danbury, Connecticut

Reading Consultants

Linda Cornwell

Coordinator of School Quality and Professional Improvement
(Indiana State Teachers Association)

Katharine A. Kane

Education Consultant
(Retired, San Diego County Office of Education and San Diego State University)

Scholastic Inc., 557 Broadway, New York, NY 10012.

Library of Congress Cataloging-in-Publication Data
Johnson, Mildred D. (Mildred Dawes)
  Wait, skates! / written by Mildred Johnson ; illustrated by Rick
Stromoski.
      p. cm. — (Rookie reader)
  Summary: A child putting on in-line roller skates for the first time
must make them wait until they are ready to go straight.
  ISBN 0-516-21640-6 (lib.bdg.)   0-516-27002-8 (pbk.)
  [1. In-line skating—Fiction. 2. Roller skating—Fiction.]
  I. Stromoski, Rick, ill. II. Title. III. Series.
PZ7.J63416Wai 1999
[E]—dc21   98-53058
                                                                 CIP
                                                                 AC

Wait!

Wait, skates!

The first time on my roller skates,

6

I tried to make my skates wait.

But they would not wait.

They went out

and sometimes in.

14

They would not wait.

They would not go straight.

But I just stopped

21

and said out loud . . .

23

24

25

27

28

Now I just sail along.

My skates go straight.

WORD LIST (30 WORDS)

along	my	stopped
and	not	straight
but	now	the
first	on	they
go	out	time
I	roller	to
in	said	tried
just	sail	wait
loud	skates	went
make	sometimes	would

ABOUT THE AUTHOR

Mildred D. Johnson is a native of Baltimore, Maryland. After moving to Chicago, she established a children's theater and continued her teaching career at Howalton School, the oldest, African-American private school in Chicago. She has conducted numerous workshops for teachers and organized many creative assemblies. Mrs. Johnson is also a playwright and the author of many children's books.

ABOUT THE ILLUSTRATOR

Rick Stromoski's award-winning cartoons and illustrations appear in national magazines, newpapers, and children's books. He lives in the historic district of Suffield, Connecticut, with his wife, Danna, and daughter, Molly.